Preface

When I was a boy, my grandmother and my martial arts teachers told me many stories. This was very common in China, especially in the old days before television and radio, and especially in previous centuries when the vast majority of the population could not read. While these stories were a main source of entertainment, they also played an important role in the moral and cultural education of the children.

These stories, many of which have been passed down by parents and grandparents to countless generations of children, have been designed or selected to give the child a sense of where he/she fits into his/her own culture and family, to encourage consideration for others, and to instill ideals and good habits. Many are designed to encourage self-confidence and the determination to persevere against adversity.

As a child I was greatly influenced by these stories, and even today they give me encouragement and help me to understand myself better. For many years I have hoped to be able to bring these stories to children in the West, both to acquaint them with Chinese culture, and to share with them the insight and encouragement that I received. I am glad to have this opportunity to share these stories, and I hope that you will come to value them as much as I do.

Dr. Yang Jwing-Ming, Ph.D.
President, YOAA, Inc.

CONTENTS

1. The Fox Borrows the Tiger's Awe

One bright summer day a clever old fox was feeling hungry. He had spent the entire morning in his cave, and so he decided to go out into the wild and catch some small animals to eat.

A short time later, as he was walking down a path, a tiger crept up from behind and caught him.

Before the tiger could eat him, the fox quickly calmed himself down and hid all of his fear. He said loudly, "Wait, tiger! Don't you know that you cannot eat me? For I was sent to the earth by heaven to rule the animal world. If you eat me, you surely will be punished by heaven!"

When the tiger heard this, he began to laugh very loud. He said, "I do not believe you, fox. You should be brave and accept your death." However, when he saw that the fox did not look terrified like all the other animals he had caught before, he became curious.

The tiger continued, "You said that you were sent by heaven to rule the animal world. Can you prove it?"

Now the fox began to think that he might escape from the jaws of this tiger. He thrust out his chest, lifted up his head and proudly proclaimed, "Yes, I was sent here by heaven to rule the animal world. If you don't believe me, then why don't we take a walk in the woods. You walk behind me and see how the other animals react when they see me coming."

The tiger was a little bit worried that perhaps the fox was telling the truth, so he decided to do what the fox had said. After all, with him walking right behind, the fox would not have a chance to escape.

And so the two of them went for a walk in the woods.

When the other animals saw the tiger as he walked behind the fox, they ran for their lives. However, to the tiger's eyes, it looked like all the animals were running away from the fox. He began to think that the fox was telling the truth, and had been sent by heaven, and he became very afraid.

Without saying a word, the tiger turned and ran away like the wind. The clever fox had saved himself from the jaws of the tiger.

Friends, very often wisdom is far more powerful than strength. Only if you study hard and keep learning will you someday be truly wise and successful.

2. A Fight of No Fight

A long time ago, there was a family that owned a small farm. The father worked very hard to make the farm successful so that he would be able to leave it to his two sons when he died. The elder son, who was married, was named Der-Shin, while the younger son, who was not married, was named Der-Yi.

One day the father became very sick, and he knew that he would soon die. He gathered his sons together and said to them, "I wish to give this farm to both of you. Share it equally, and help each other to make it successful. I hope that it makes you as happy as it has made me." With these words the father quietly passed away.

The sons divided the land equally and set about the task of building their own farms. Even though they had divided the land, they still cooperated, helping each other with the more difficult chores.

However, not long after the father died, Der-Shin's wife decided that she and Der-Shin had not received enough land. After all, Der-Yi was single and didn't need as much land as they did. So she began urging her husband to request more land from his brother.

Finally, after considerable provoking from his wife, Der-Shin demanded more land from Der-Yi. Because Der-Shin was much bigger and stronger, the only thing Der-Yi could do was to concede in angry silence, and let his brother occupy more land.

However, Der-Shin's wife was still not satisfied. When she saw how easy it was to get more land from her brother-in-law, she again urged her husband to demand more land. Again, Der-Yi could only consent to his brother's demands. Still Der-Shin's wife was not satisfied, and finally she demanded that Der-Yi leave all the land to her and her husband.

22

Der-Yi requested help from his relatives and friends, and begged them to mediate the conflict. None would help. They knew it was unfair for Der-Yi to be forced off his land, but they were afraid because they knew of Der-Shin's violent temper.

Finally, Der-Yi decided to take a stand for what he knew was right. He decided to stay, even though his brother wanted him to leave. For this defiance Der-Shin beat him very, very badly. Der-Yi was finally forced to leave his home and become a traveling street beggar.

One day, while traveling in the Jeou Lien Mountain region of Fujian province, he saw several Shaolin priests in town on an expedition to purchase food. He knew that the Shaolin monks were good in Kung Fu, and he thought that if he could learn Kung Fu he could beat Der-Shin and regain the land that was rightfully his.

He decided to follow the
monks, and when they reached
the temple he would request that
they take him as a student of
Kung Fu.

When they arrived at the
temple he requested to see the
Head Priest.

The Head Priest welcomed him, and asked him why he had requested the meeting. Der-Yi told the Head Priest his sad story, and asked to be taught Kung Fu so that he could regain his land.

The Head Priest looked at him, pondered for a few minutes, and finally said, "Der-Yi, if you are willing to endure the painfully hard training, then you are accepted as a student here." With deep appreciation, Der-Yi knelt down and bowed to the Head Priest.

Early the next morning, Der-Yi was summoned to the back yard. The Head Priest was standing in front of a young willow tree, holding a calf. He said to Der-Yi, "Before you learn any Kung Fu you must first build up your strength. To do this you must hold this calf in your arms and jump over this willow tree fifty times in the morning and fifty times in the evening." Der-Yi replied, "Yes, master. This is a simple task and I will do it every day."

From then on, Der-Yi held the calf in his arms and jumped over the willow tree every morning and every night.

Days passed, weeks passed, months passed, and years passed. The calf grew into a cow and the small willow tree grew into a big tree. Still, Der-Yi held the cow in his arms and jumped over the tree.

One day, he requested to see the Head Priest. He asked, "Dear Master, I have held the cow and jumped over the willow tree for three years already. Do you think I am strong enough to train Kung Fu?"

The Head Priest looked at him and the cow. He smiled and said, "Der-Yi, you do not have to learn anymore. You have completed your Kung Fu training. Your strength is enough to regain your lost land. You should take this cow home with you and use it to cultivate your land."

Der-Yi looked at the Head Priest with surprise and asked, "If I have not learned any martial arts, what do I do if my brother comes to fight me again for my land?" The Head Priest laughed and said, "Do not worry, Der-Yi. If your brother comes to fight you again, simply pick up the cow and run towards him. There will be no fight."

Der-Yi half-believed the Head Priest, but he also thought that perhaps the Head Priest was joking with him. He took the cow and left the Shaolin Temple. When he arrived home, he started to cultivate his land.

Der-Shin soon discovered his brother's return. He decided to beat up his young brother again and teach him an unforgettable lesson. After that, Der-Yi would never dare to return.

When Der-Yi came to the rice field, he saw his brother running towards him, shouting in anger.

When Der-Yi saw his brother running towards him, he remembered what the Head Priest had said and immediately picked up the cow and ran towards his brother.

This surprised and shocked Der-Shin. He just could not believe that his brother possessed such strength. He turned around and ran away, never to return again.

Friends, this story has two lessons. The first is that you need patience and endurance to succeed. Big successes always come from many little efforts. The second lesson is that the best way to win a fight is without fighting. Often you can win a fight with wisdom, and this is better than beating someone up.

3. A Rich Man in Jail

Once upon a time there was a man who worked very hard. Day and night he worked, and he gradually became richer and richer. However, as the days went by and as his pile of money grew, he also began to worry more and more. He worried about how to make more money, and he worried about how to keep both friends and enemies away so that he could safely enjoy all his money.

As time went on, he made the fence around his house higher and higher, and he made the walls of his house thicker and thicker. He put strong locks on all of his doors, and he even put bars in all of the windows. After a time, the house looked more like a jail than a house. However, the man was happy, because he finally felt safe. All day long he counted his money, and considered himself the richest and happiest man in the whole world.

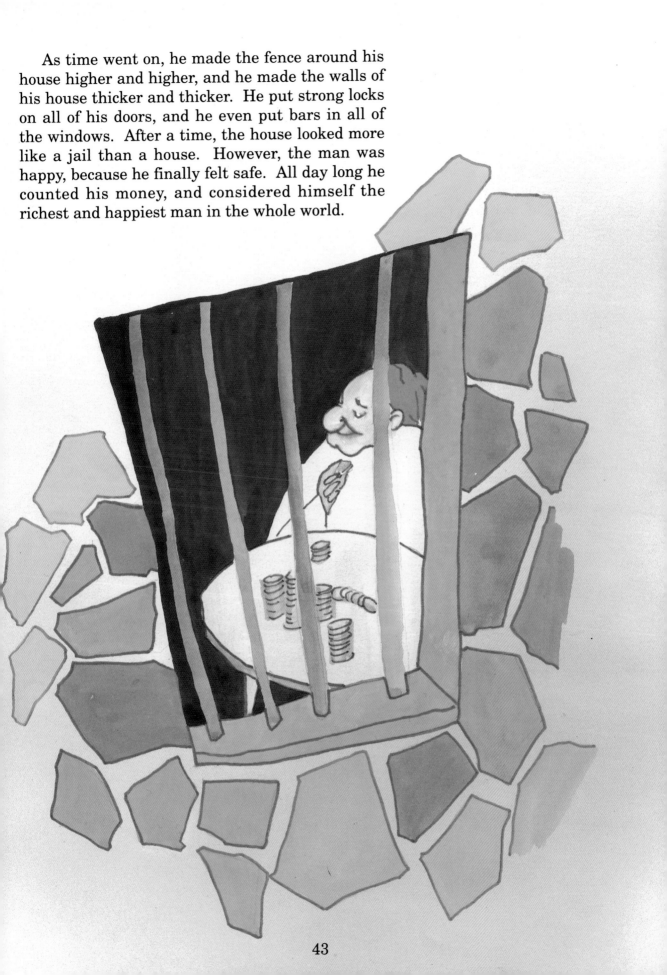

One day another man was passing by, and he stopped and looked in the window of the house. He saw the man sitting there with a big smile on his face, counting his money. The man looking in the window said, "Hey mister, why are you so happy? You're in jail!"

But the man inside answered, "No! No! It is not that I am in the jail, it is that you are outside of the jail!"

Friends, many people dream only of money. Because of this, they gradually build invisible jails so that they can enjoy themselves and keep their friends and enemies away. Do you do this? What do you think it means to be really happy and rich? Someone who is truly rich is rich both in money and spirit.

4. The Trick of Gold

A long time ago there was an old master who could change an ordinary rock into a piece of gold.

Many poor people came to him and asked if he had any extra little pieces of gold lying around that they might have. The kind old man never disappointed them, and he helped them all as much as he could.

One day, a twelve year old boy came to see him. The boy said, "Honorable master, I heard that you can change a rock into a piece of gold. Is this true?"

The old master replied, "Yes, it is. Do you want a piece of gold like the others? If you do, I will change a rock into gold for you."

"Oh no, honorable master," said the boy, "I do not want the gold. What I would like from you, if you permit, is your trick for changing rocks into gold."

The master realized that this boy was different from all the others, and he smiled. The boy had realized that if the old man gave him a piece of gold, it would soon be spent. However, if he knew how to make the gold himself, he would have enough gold for the rest of his life.

Friends, when you are learning something, what do you aim for? Do you just want quick results, or do you look for the way to get the best results in the long run? When you see flowers or eat fruit, what do you think of? Do you just notice how beautiful the flowers are, and how sweet the fruit is, or do you think of how you can grow them?

Carving the Buddha

Also Inside!

Hou Yi Learns Archery

The Mask of the King

Also Inside!

A Blessing in Disguise

The Poison of Love

The Thief and the Bell